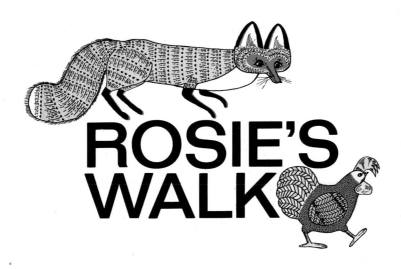

ROSIE'S
WALK

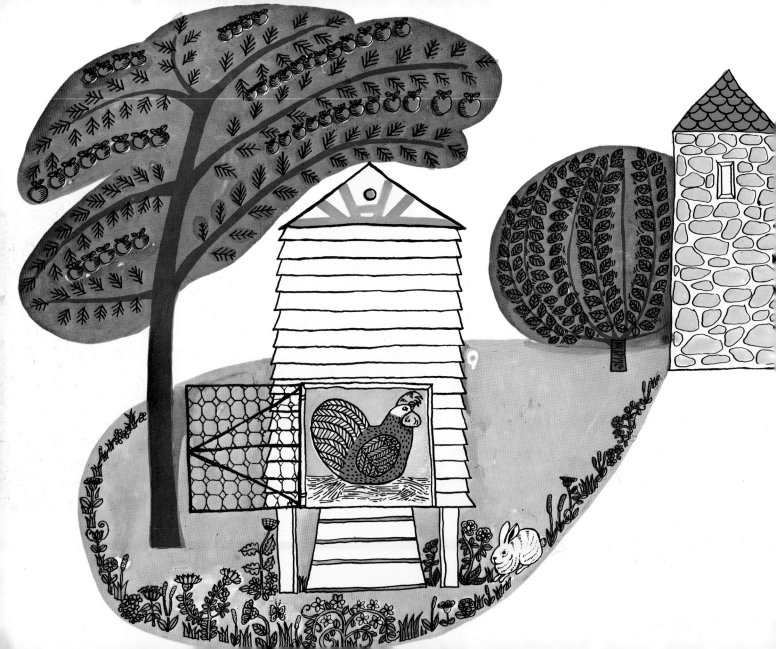

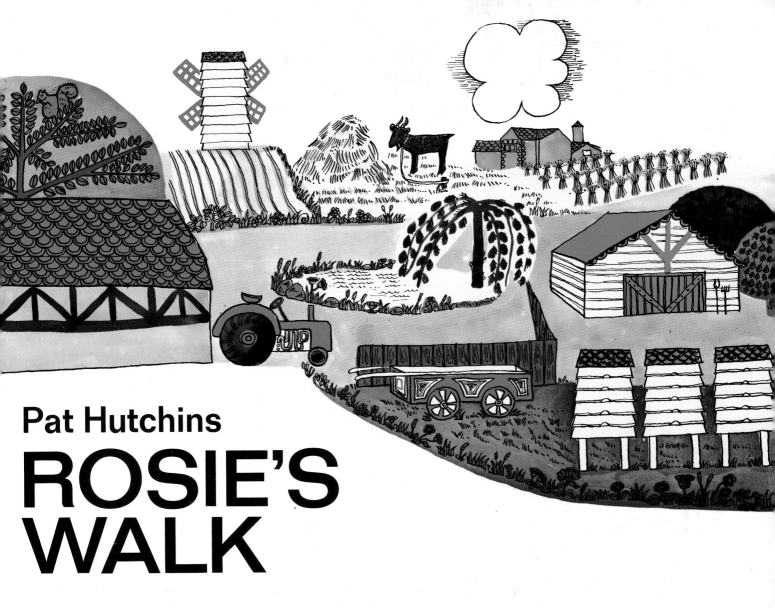

Pat Hutchins

ROSIE'S WALK

PUFFIN BOOKS

For
Wendy
and
Stephen

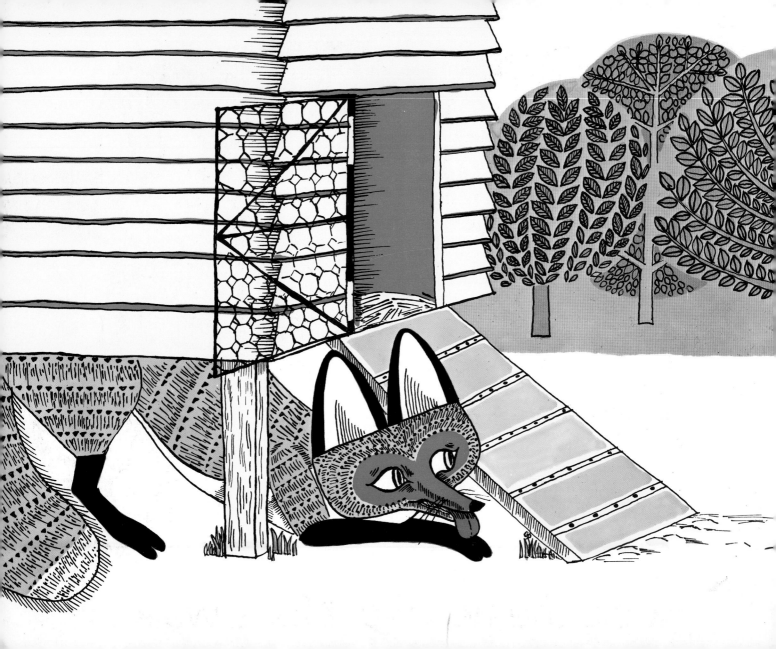

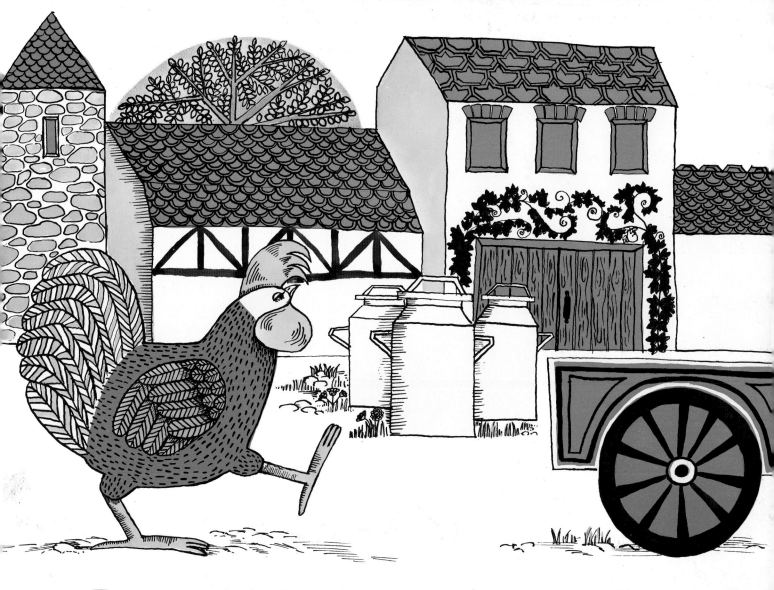

Rosie the hen went for a walk

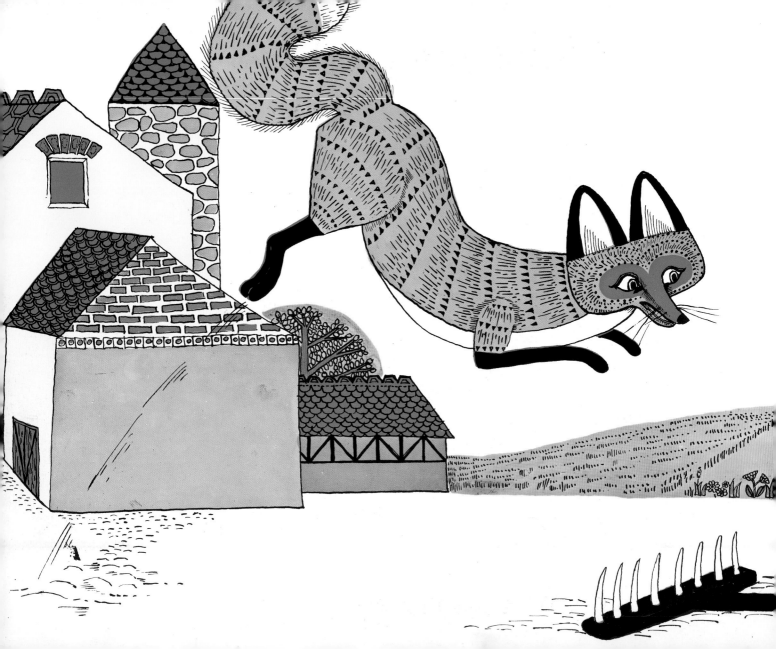

across the yard

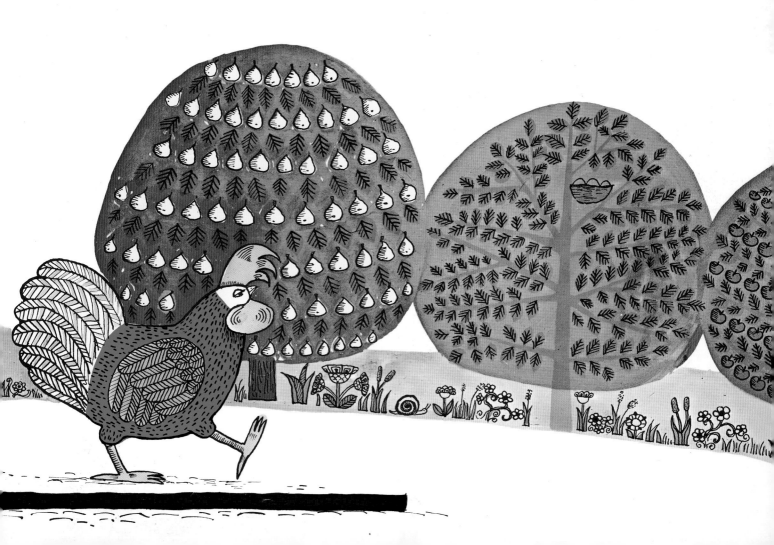

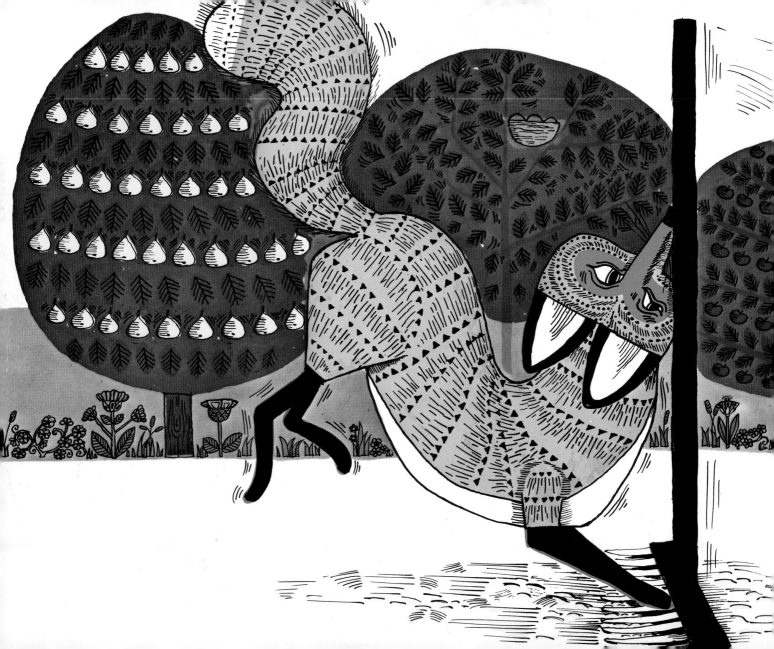

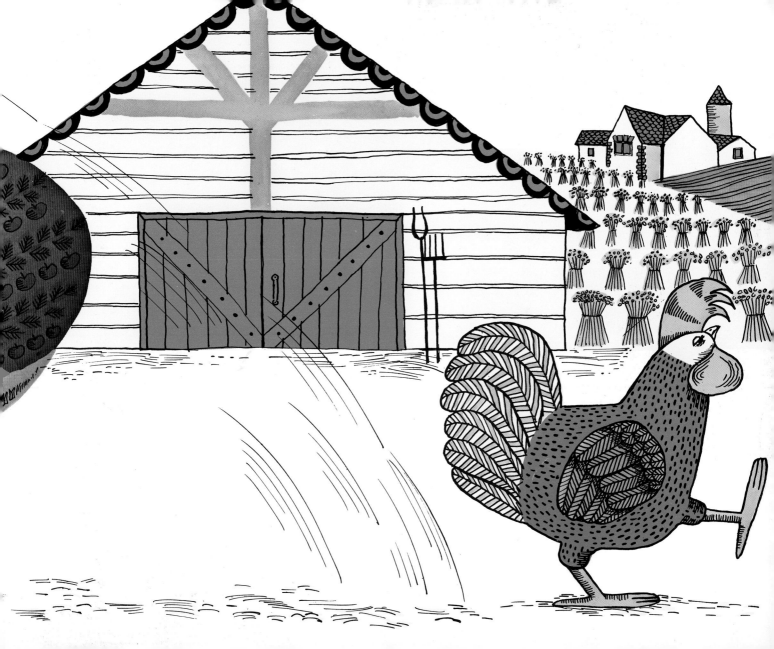

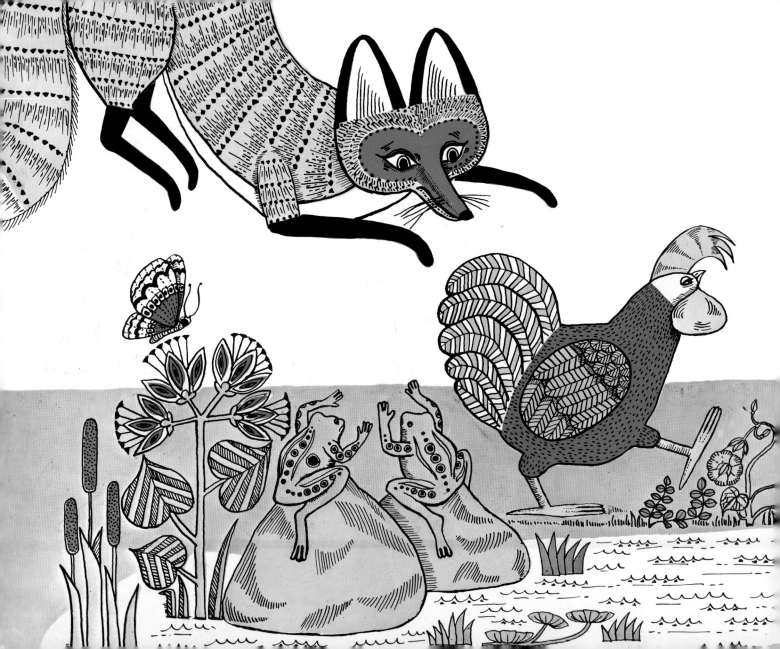

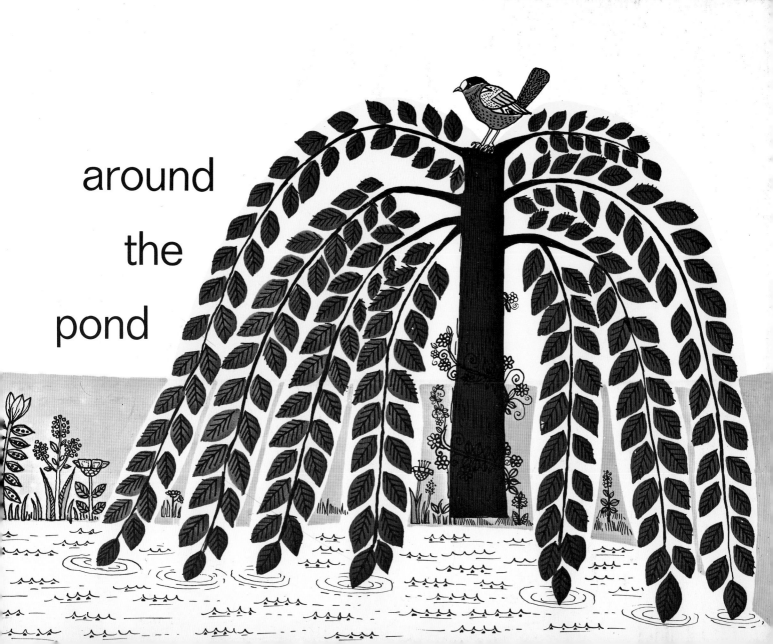

around

the

pond

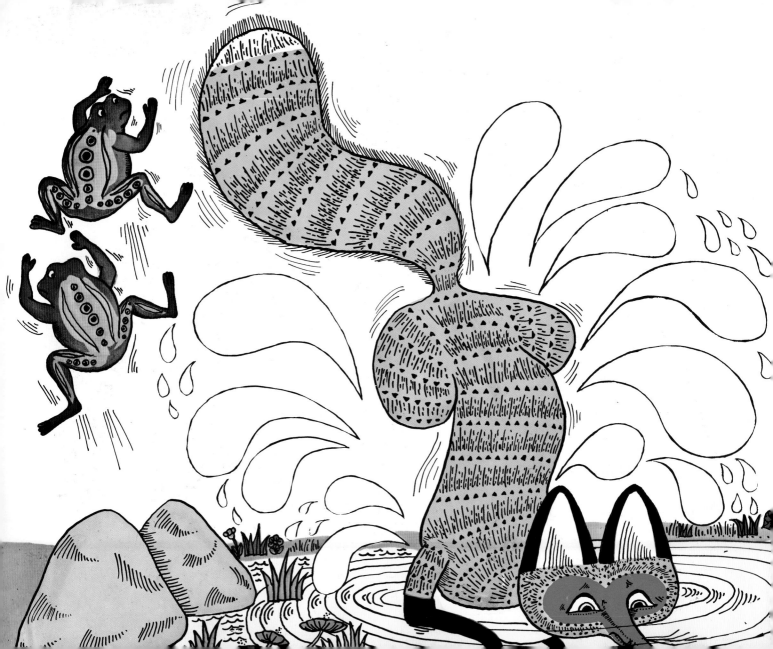

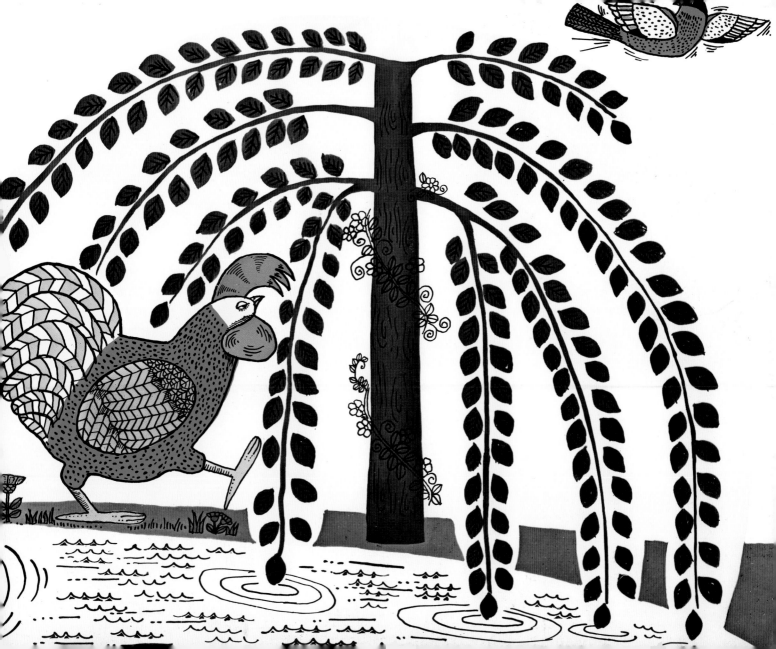

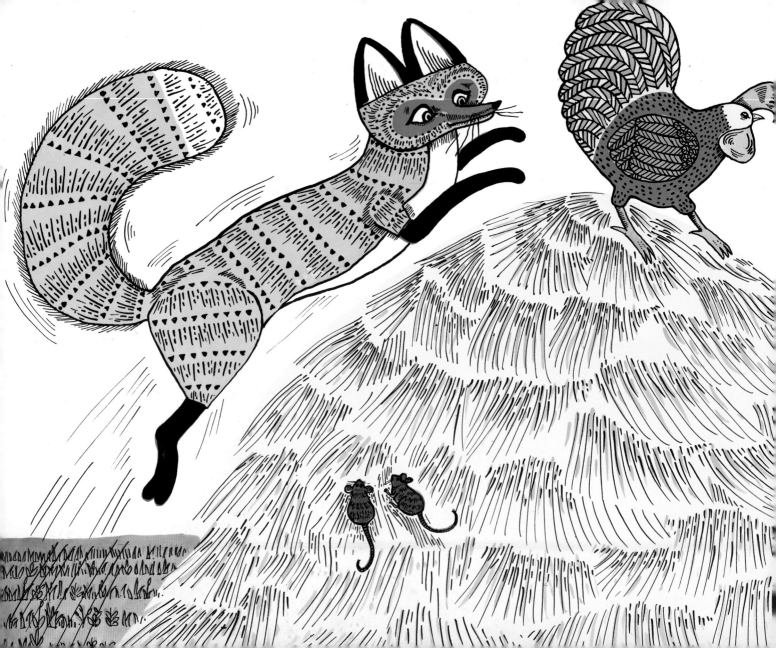

over the haycock

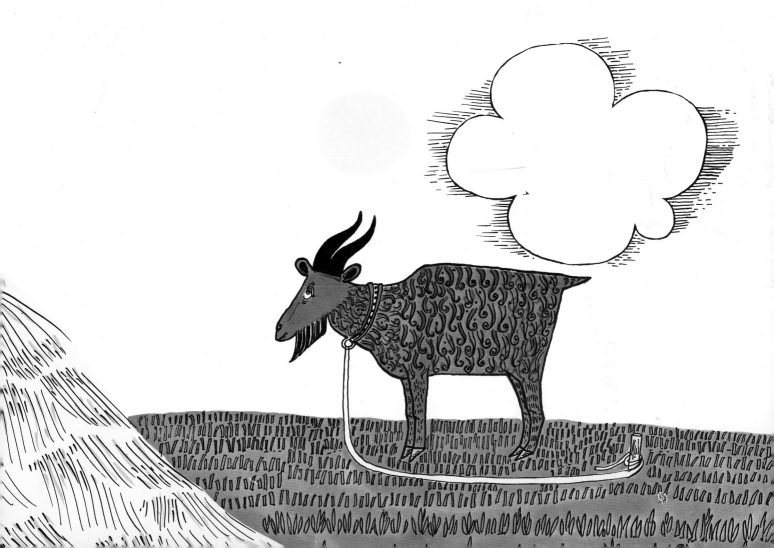

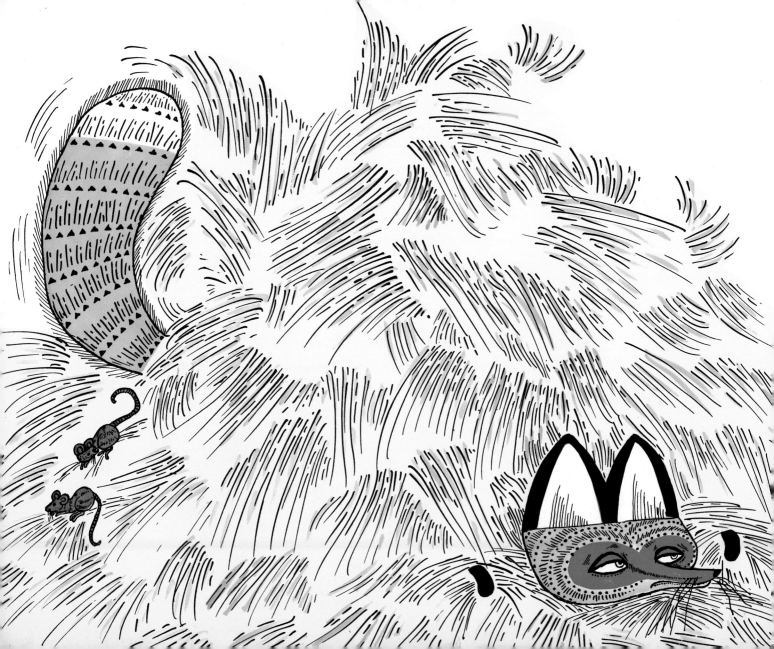

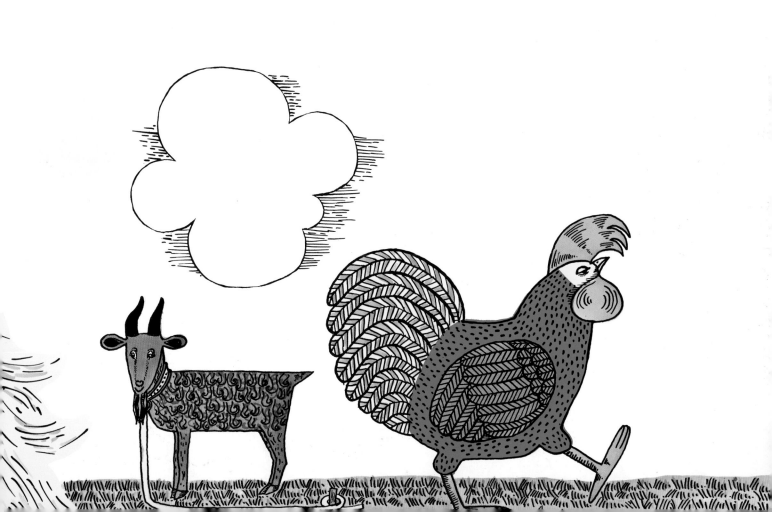

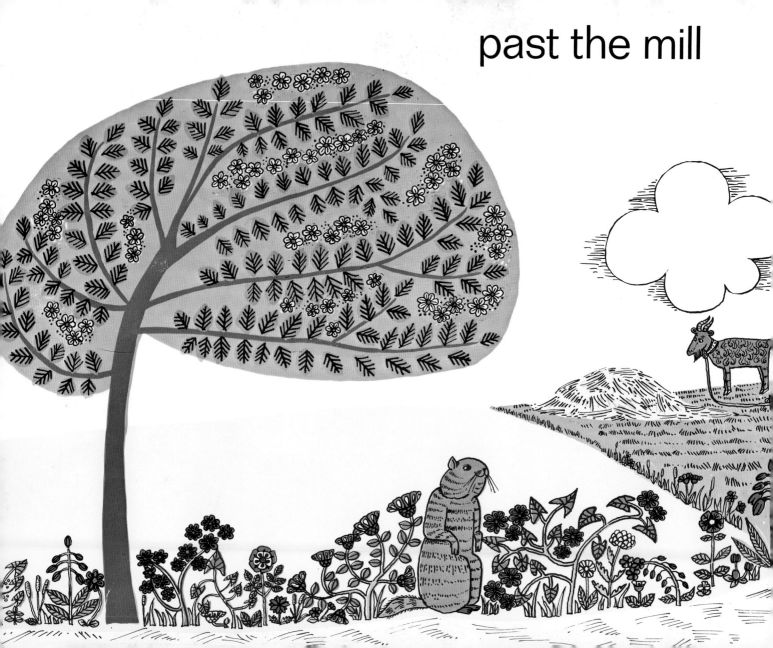

past the mill

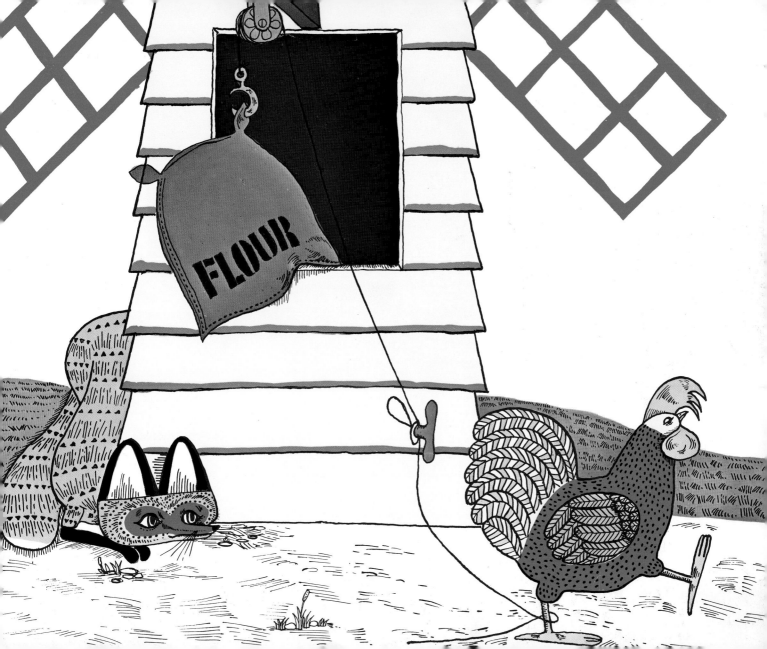

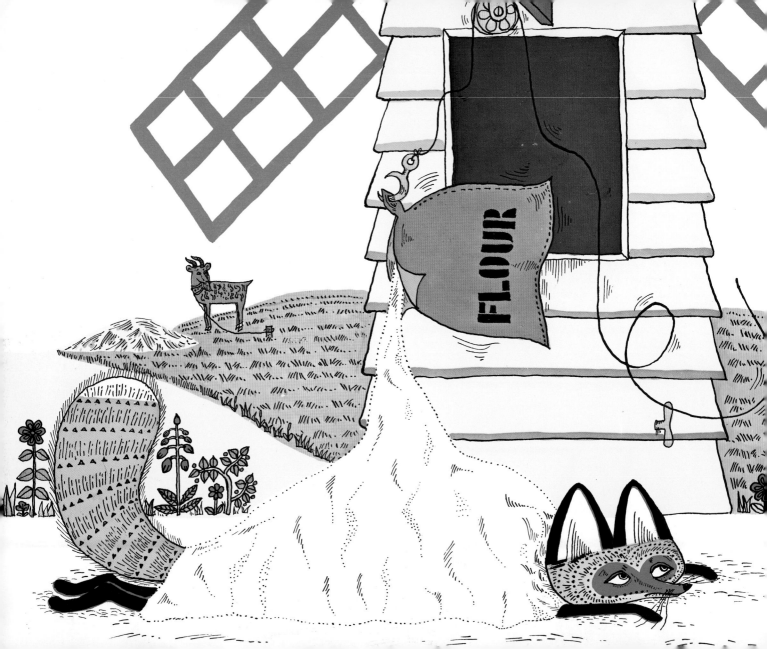

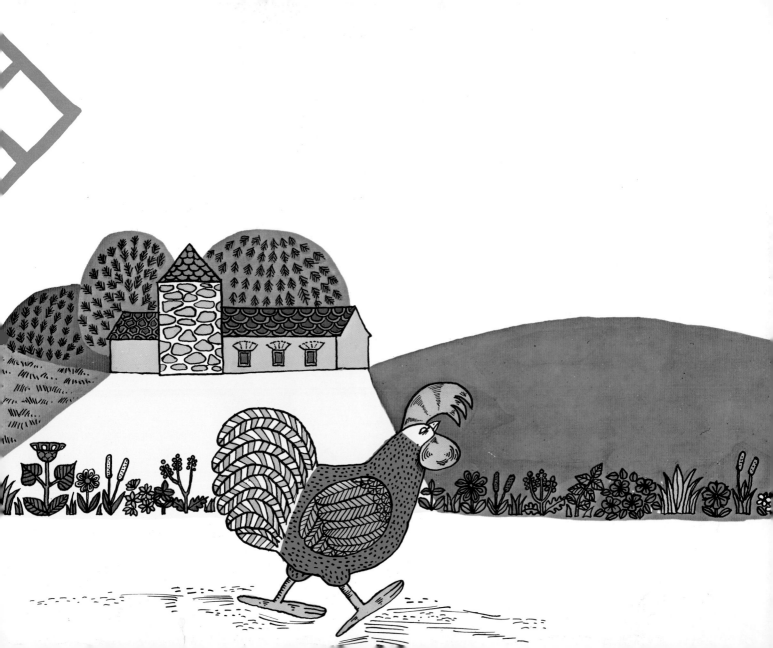

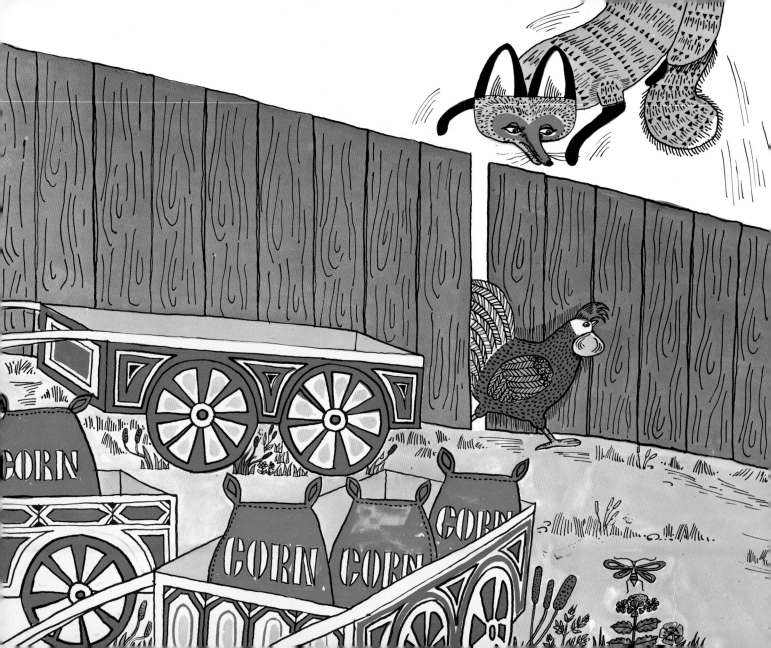

through the fence

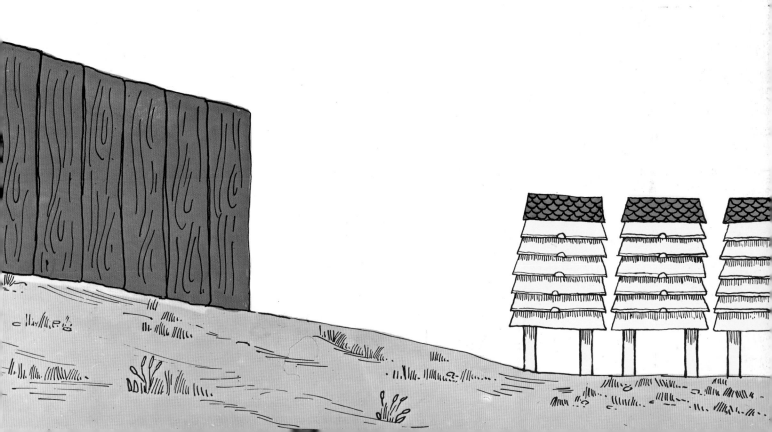

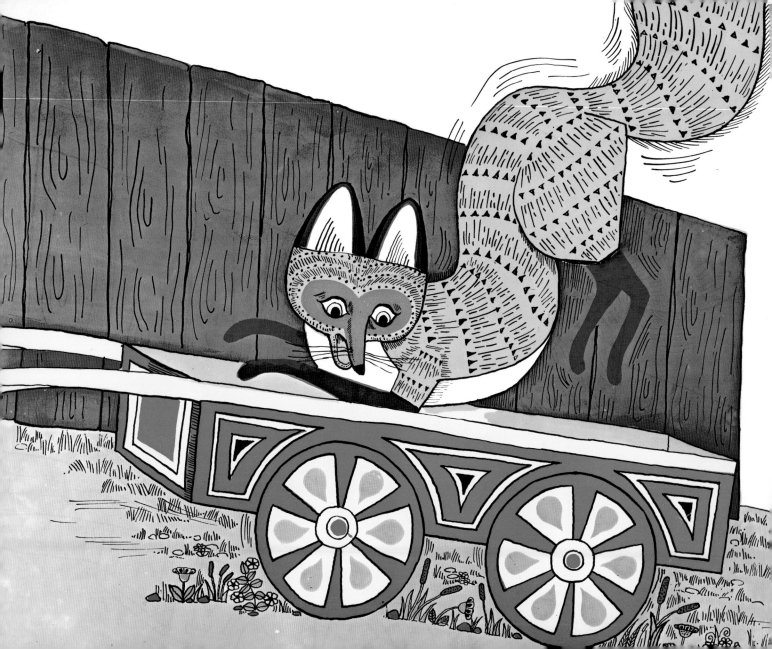

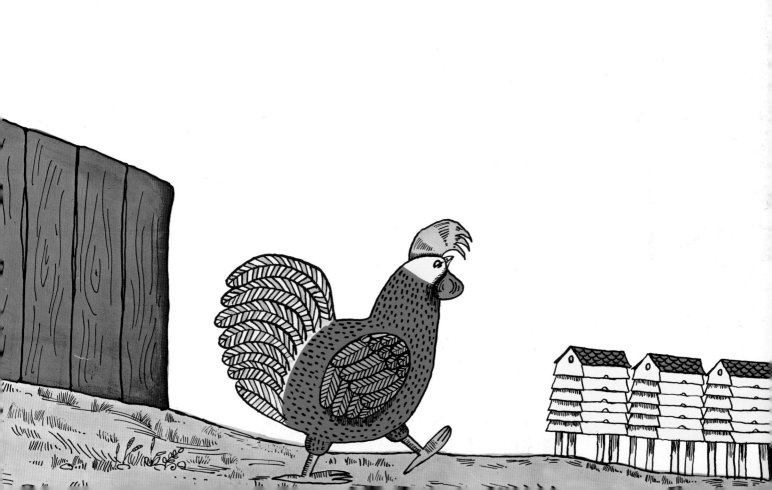

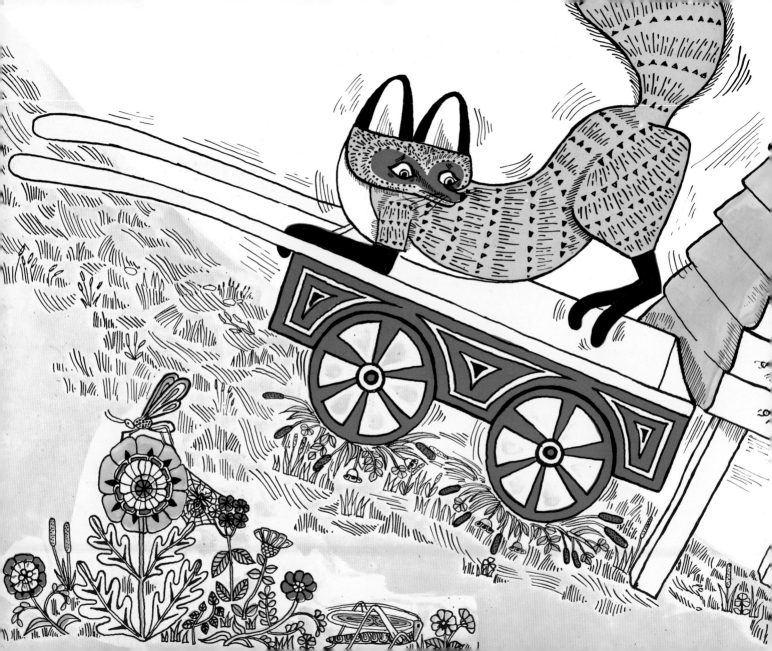

under the beehives

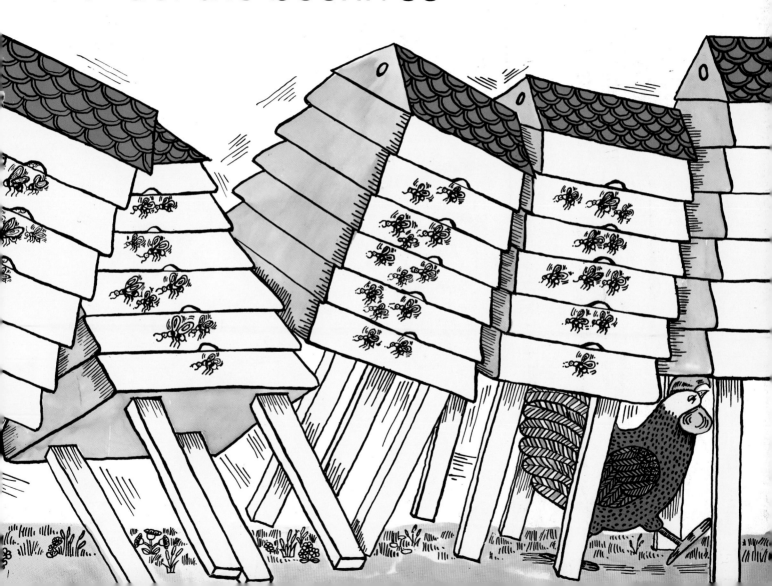

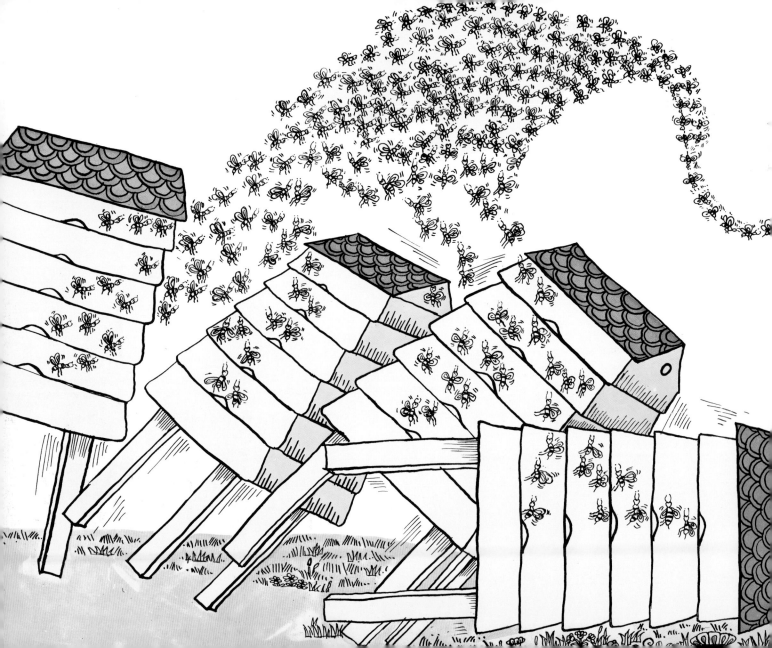

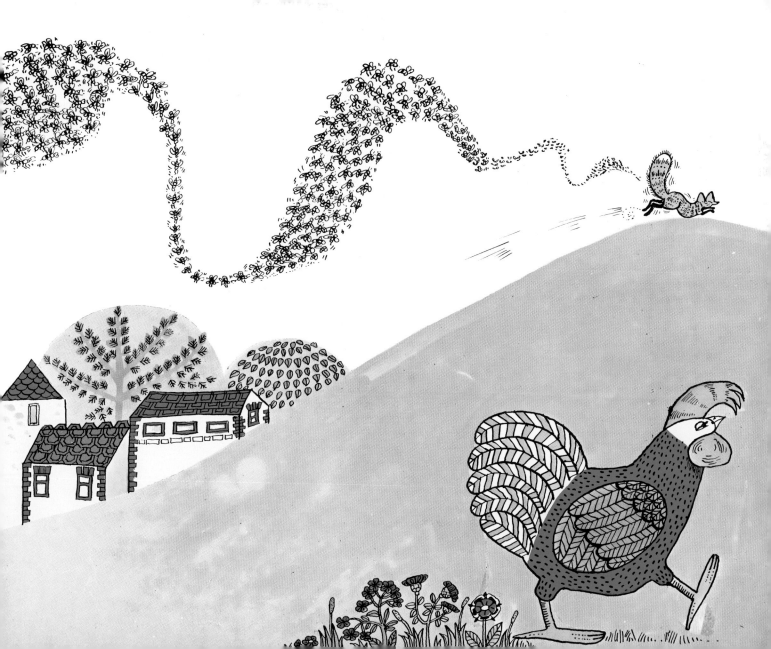

and
got back
in time
for dinner.

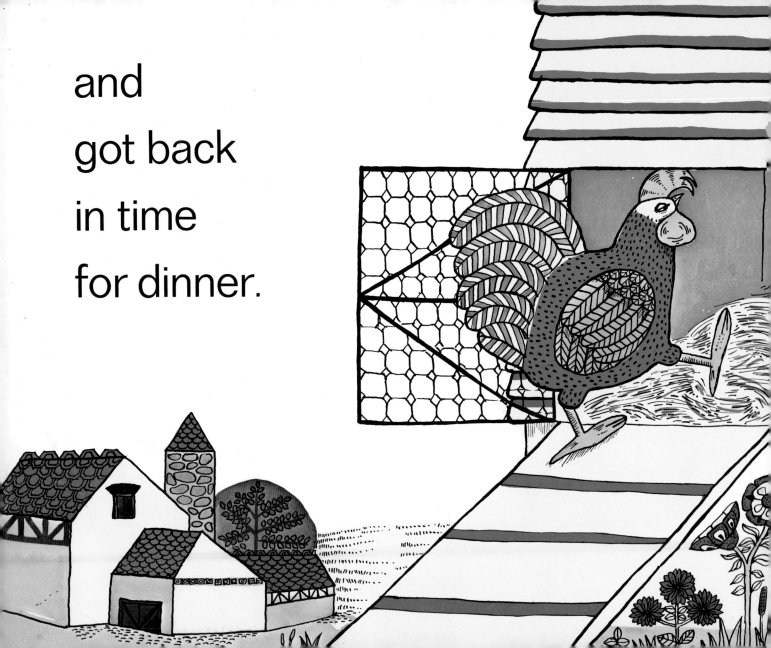